CHAMPION

A BBW & BAD BOY ROMANCE

LANA LOVE

LOVE HEART BOOKS

For more Lana Love books, please visit:

https://www.amazon.com/Lana-Love/e/B078KKRB1T/

https://www.loveheartbooks.com

CHAPTER 1

"Girl, he's never going to ask you out. You need to ask him first. My brother is way too hardheaded for his own good. I know you've seen that by now." Beth pauses, wiping her mouth with her napkin.

"I don't know, Beth. He only sees me as his employee." I sigh and shake my head. "It seemed like a good plan, but I haven't seen even a flicker of interest." I can't hide my disappointment. Beth and Shelly assured me that being around Champ would get him to notice me. "I'm not sure this matchmaking is working."

"Give it time, Opal," Beth advises. "I know how you feel about him. Lord knows what you see in that stubborn brother of mine, but if you see it, it's worth fighting for."

I smile and nod. Champ isn't like any man I've dated in the past. My friends are all crashing through life and enjoying dating strings of men, but that's not what I want. I want a man who's stable and kind. Champ may be a little older than me, but he draws me to him like the strongest magnet on earth—I just want to be with him.

Champ has his life together, but it's more than that. Every time I see him, he radiates goodness. There's no denying he's intense and can be a complete grump, but even that is sexy. He makes me feel safe. It's not that I've had an unstable life, but he protects those he loves and is a rock of reliability.

"You should ask him out," Beth says, interrupting my thoughts. "He's dense enough to miss what's right in front of his face. And don't let him feed you some bull line about him not dating. He may act like a monk, but I know he's not happy. That's why your sister and I got this idea. You're crushing on him, and he needs a woman. His needing a second bookkeeper for the new gym was the icing on the cake, giving you a way to spend time together and get to know each other."

"Then what do you suggest I do? I can't just ask him to dinner and a movie." I motion to the waitress to bring our check. I'd love to spend the afternoon with her, but this lunch is all we have time for. She has to get back to the bank and I'm due back at the gym here in Raytown.

"Yeah, you're right that you can't be that direct. Invite him to something else. Oh! I have it!" Beth lifts a napkin and wipes her mouth. "Invite him to the chili cook-off this weekend."

"I thought we were going to that?" I tilt my head. We've been planning to go for weeks because my friend, Rebecca, has entered the competition, and we want to support her.

"No. I'll tell a fib and say I can't go. Then you can invite him because you'll have an extra ticket. It's perfect! He already supports Warrior Cares, so the cook-off benefit will be a draw for him."

I consider Beth's suggestion. She has a point. Champ is a vet and big on community. A flicker of hope rises in me. "That may work." I push my doubts aside and smile.

"But we should stage it," Beth adds quickly. "I'll call you Friday afternoon, so it'll seem like a last-minute cancellation from me. I'll say I'm not feeling up to it or something."

"Won't he get worried if you say you're not feeling well?"

"I doubt it. If he asks, I'll say I'm having bad cramps or whatever. Dirk doesn't have a fight coming up, so he can pamper me." Beth's smile is filled with confidence in her plan.

A thread of optimism pulls at me. "Okay. Let's do it."

* * *

I STAND in the doorway of my office, scanning the gym for Champ. Finally spotting him, I wave him over to the office. "I need to talk to you!" I have a printout of this week's bank transactions, which he needs to explain.

"Yeah, Opal. What do you need?" Champ drapes a towel around his neck.

I have to focus on *not* staring at the popping muscles in his arms. "Champ, what are these cash withdrawals? I need to know so I can reconcile them properly."

He stares at me blankly. I sigh and hand him a printout of the bank statement. "You've taken out nearly four-thousand dollars. I need to know what you're using it for."

"They're expenses," he barks as if that explains everything. Champ crosses his muscular arms over his chest, his body tense.

"That doesn't help. What are you using this money *for*?"

Champ stares at me, but his dark brown eyes reveal nothing. "Stuff."

"What stuff?" I ask, exasperated. It shouldn't be that hard to say what this money is for.

"None of your business."

Champ turns and walks away, leaving me stunned as I watch him get back in the ring with Dirk. He's gruff, but he's always been open and honest with me. Why doesn't he understand that it is my business if he expects me to be his bookkeeper?

* * *

By the time Friday rolls around, I'm convinced this matchmaking thing is a terrible idea, and nothing will ever happen. Ever since I asked Champ about the cash withdrawals, he's been avoiding me. I'm too tired to keep playing a game like this. Between school and work, and the days I have to come here from Jefferson, I'm exhausted. Moving to Jefferson to be closer to school was supposed to reduce my commute time.

Beth keeps telling me I need to take the initiative with Champ, but he's holding back, not to mention he's my boss. I don't get any encouragement or warmth to suggest he may be interested.

"You're probably overthinking things," I tell myself. But it's hard not to. I'm attracted to Champ in a way I've never been attracted to any other man. I love being around him, even if we're not talking.

But I also know that if a man's not going to pay attention to me, then it's a fool's game to keep pining after him. I figure that once Shelly has everything set up at the new gym, I'll transfer over there, and then I won't have to see Champ very often. This job is good for my resume, and I'm getting college credit for it. But I remind myself this is a job, first and foremost, regardless of Beth and Shelly trying to set me up with Champ.

My phone buzzes with a text message, and I know what I'm going to see when I pick it up.

Sorry, I can't make it tonight. Beth writes. My stomach hasn't been feeling great, so I'm going to have a quiet night in. I hope Rebecca wins the chili cook-off!

That's a bummer. I hope you feel better soon! I text back.

I put my phone face down on my desk, and butterflies fill my stomach when I see Champ watching me from across the gym. Every time I convince myself I need to ignore how I feel around Champ, it all goes out the window when he looks at me.

Calm down, Opal. I tell myself.

I return my focus to the pile of invoices next to me and make sure they're taken care of before my shift ends. Champ always says I can head out when I'm finished instead of sitting around when there's nothing to do. If nothing else, tonight is Friday, and I'd rather go and hang out with Rebecca than stay here at the gym.

"Hey, Opal. You doing okay in here? You've been quiet." I startle as Champ fills the doorway.

“Oh, I'm okay. Beth was supposed to go with me to the chili cook-off tonight. You know, the one to benefit Warrior Cares? She said she wasn't feeling well.”

“Is she okay?” he asks, concern filling his face.

“Oh, um, lady stuff.” I glance away, suddenly awkward. I don’t like lying and hadn’t considered that I would be the one sharing Beth’s white lie.

Champ nods but doesn’t leave the office. “Look. I’m sorry I was short with you the other day. I didn’t mean to be rude about the cash withdrawals. Can you just put it under something personal?”

“Like personal expenses? I still need receipts.”

Champ frowns. “I’ll see what I can do.”

I look at him for a long moment, a surge of bravery filling me. “Hey. You don’t have to say yes, but with Beth staying home tonight, I now have an extra ticket for the chili cook-off. Would you like to join me?”

Champ blinks and looks at me in surprise. “Opal, that’s a kind offer, but I think I’ll pass.”

“Are you sure?” I ask, pressing on. “My friend, Rebecca, is competing with her grandfather’s secret recipe. It’s delicious.” I smile, hoping Champ will change his mind.

He gives me a long look, but his face doesn’t reveal his thoughts. ”I may consider it,” he finally says.

His expression softens as he looks at me, but I don’t know if it’s my kindness in offering him a ticket or if he’s letting his guard down and maybe I have a chance with him.

"Okay, well, I'm going to leave the ticket here on the desk, so if you change your mind, come and find me."

Champ nods and watches me prop the ticket against the base of the new computer monitor before returning to the gym floor.

It always seems like I watch him walk away from me.

I chide myself for being dramatic, but I can't help how I react to Champ. While it's great to be close to him when I'm filling in for Shelly, it's also torture when he has such high walls around him. At first, I thought working in the Jefferson gym when it opens would be worse, but now I think it'll be a blessing. Who wants to be around someone who resists them?

Get it together, Opal.

My brother would kill me if he knew how I felt about Champ, but it's none of his business. Champ would have kittens if he knew who my brother was. It's something I plan on keeping secret for as long as possible.

CHAPTER 2

"Don't do this to me!" I warn my truck as I pull up to a stoplight.

The truck is shuddering again. I've been meaning to take it to the shop, but running between the gym and the new place in Jefferson has kept me busy. I hope it doesn't break down on me. Fortunately, I get home without incident and unload all the supplies I bought for Harley into my garage.

After I close up the garage, I call Harley on the phone as I walk back into my house. "Hey, Harley, I'm all stocked up. Let me know when you arrive at the mountain, and I'll head up so I can deliver all these things to you."

"Sounds good, man. I appreciate it. I hope to see you. I may have to head out as soon as I drop the women off, so I'm not sure if our paths will cross." Harley sounds relieved.

"Well, I hope it works out we see each other," I say. "It's been too long since we talked. Though I can't talk long now. I've got to get back to the gym. I'm having an issue with a boxer and need to see where we're at with him."

"No worries, man. I'll see you when I see ya, but it'll be soon."

"Right, man. Later."

Driving back to the gym, my truck is fine. Maybe it's nothing, though my inner voice tells me I'm fooling myself.

"Hey, Champ, how's it hangin'?" Dirk asks, coming up to me as I enter the gym.

I grimace as I see Mannie, yet again, acting like a clown in the ring. That dimwit is going to get seriously hurt if he keeps this shit up.

"Didn't I ask you to talk to Mannie?" I ask Dirk, rolling my eyes.

"You thought I was a showboater and didn't want to devote myself to the sport," he says. I'm not liking the sound of where this is going. "Mannie is a hundred times worse than I was, Champ, and I did talk to him like you asked," Dirk says. "But he's even more hardheaded than you are."

"Watch your tone, Dirk. You may be my brother-in-law, but don't push me."

"Yeah, yeah. Whatever, Champ," Dirk laughs. His smile fades when he turns back to the ring and watches Mannie. "I know you don't like cutting boxers loose, Champ, but I think you gotta do it. He won't listen to instructions. He's gonna get hurt, not to mention he'll damage the gym's reputation."

I sigh. This is the hard part of running my gym. I don't tolerate fools or boxers unwilling to work on their craft. I don't want any of my boys getting injured, and if Mannie isn't following the rules, he's a liability I can't have. You can only tell somebody so many times before you realize they're never going to listen and they're willfully going to do precisely what you've told them not to.

“Alright,” I sigh, “I want you to have a talk with him later. Either he shapes up, or he's outta here. No exceptions. Be clear this is his second and final chance.”

Dirk sighs, then nods. I still give him shit because what kind of a big brother would I be if I didn't disapprove of my little sis's choice in men? But Dirk is becoming someone I can rely on. I have my eye on him to look after this gym when I'm out in Jefferson, training those boxers after it opens up.

I respect his commitment and dedication to the gym and do my best to ensure he knows.

“You're a good man, Dirk,” I say, looking at him with pride.

Who thought Dirk would be the one I considered my right-hand man here at the gym? It's certainly been a welcome surprise and improved my relationship with my sister.

“Anyway, what are you up to this weekend?” Dirk asks, curious. It still seems strange to shoot the shit with him, but now that he's settled down with my sister, he's found a purpose in life, and we have better common ground.

“Me?” I shrug, downplaying his question. “Not sure. Opal has invited me to the chili cook-off, but...”

“Oh, did she now?” Dirk gives me a shit-eating grin like he knows something I don't.

“What's that supposed to mean? What do you know?” I ask, glowering at him. I don't like being at a disadvantage, especially with Dirk.

“Nothing specific,” he says, running his hand through his hair. “But I overheard Beth and Shelly talking, and they're up to something. I'm pretty sure Opal's in the middle of it.”

I look at Dirk and realize this is exactly the kind of thing my sister would do. Like I need another thing on my plate to deal with.

“But what do you think about her, Champ?” Dirk asks. “You're always single. Maybe it's time for you to settle down. It's not hard to see that she wants you to notice her.”

“No, no, that's not for me,” I say quickly, working to shake the image of Opal from my head. My mission in life is to help other people, and it's something I give everything to. I'm no fool. I've seen the way Opal looks at me. There's no denying she's a beautiful woman, but she's off-limits. “Besides, she's my employee. That's its own set of problems.”

“Yeah, whatever you say, man.” Dirk smirks, clearly not believing me. “I'm going back to training, but catch you later, yeah? I'll talk to Mannie again.”

“Thanks.”

I head into the office and sit at the desk. Truth be told, I've liked having Opal around. Having Opal here is different from Beth or Shelly. Beth is a pain in my ass most of the time, no matter how much I love my sister. Shelly is all business, and she's been wonderful. She's blossomed now she's away from her abusive ex and is madly in love with Floyd. She's no longer the timid and terrified woman I met earlier this year.

But Opal? Opal's got these soft curves and this sweet smile, and I'd be lying if I said I didn't think about her at night when I'm in bed. It's hard to ignore Opal, but as her boss, I force myself to ignore her sweet smiles and the hopeful way she looks at me. But I'm not a fool. I've noticed the changes in her, like wearing dresses to the gym. It makes me wonder if she's trying to catch someone's eye. I'd like to believe she's been making an effort for me, but I keep telling myself it was foolish to hire her in the first place.

Hiring Opal was good for the gym but bad for me. Every time she walks in, my body floods with longing. But as much as I want her, I know better than to cross that line with an employee. No matter what I feel, I have to keep my distance. Between running this gym, getting ready to open the one in Jefferson, and helping Harley, there isn't enough space in my life for a woman, no matter how much Opal intrigues me.

Dammit, Champ. This is the last thing you need. You don't need the complication of a relationship, no matter how much you like Opal.

There are so many reasons why something like that can go wrong. Not like asking an employee on a date is ever a good idea. Besides, I've heard her say she has a few brothers, and the last thing I need is to be chased around by a bunch of angry older brothers.

I chuckle to myself. That's exactly what I did with Dirk when he started sniffing after Beth. My eyes fall to the desk, and I see the ticket for the cook-off that Opal left me. Maybe I'll go, I tell myself. It's a fundraiser, not a date. There will be other people around, and it's in support of Warrior Cares, an organization I deeply believe in.

As I pick up the ticket and put it carefully in my wallet, I realize I'm fooling myself. Maybe Dirk's right, and it is time for me to settle down. But why would a sweet young girl like Opal want a grizzled old grump like me?

CHAPTER 3

"Why do you keep looking around?" My friend Rebecca asks.

I stand with my friend as she gives out samples of her chili. So far, people love the chili, and it looks like she'll at least place in the competition.

"I'm just watching the crowd, seeing who's here," I say, trying to be vague as I scan people's faces.

Rebecca looks at me, her blue eyes narrowing. "Opal Malone, what aren't you telling me? Are you looking for somebody specific? I know you were supposed to come with Beth, but didn't you say she was sick?"

"I did, but she's not really sick. I saw her the other day, and she's fine. It's just…"

"Just what?" Rebecca prompts.

"Beth and Shelly are trying to set me up with Beth's brother."

“They're trying to set you up with Champ? I thought he was a mean old bastard.”

“No.” I sigh. One of the things I like about him is that he doesn’t put on a ‘nice’ face just because that’s what people say you should do. “He's gruff and can be a grump, but he's got a good heart.”

“If you say so,” Rebecca says, looking at me doubtfully, then grins. “Opal, do you have a *crush* on Champ?”

“Maybe a little bit,” I concede, feeling a blush color my cheeks. “Beth said I should invite him, so I did. I left Beth’s ticket for him in the office, but I don’t think he's coming.” I say, disappointment in my voice.

“Well, he would be lucky to have you, Opal.”

“Thanks. But what about you? How are you feeling about your chances with the chili?”

“I think I have a good shot,” she says, lighting up with excitement. “You’ve seen how people are reacting to Grandad’s chili. My biggest competition is old man Denton. He's won this for so many years. But I don't know, Opal – maybe I have a chance?”

“You do, Rebecca. Your grandfather's recipe is amazing. You’re giving Denton a run for his money.”

“I hope so.” Rebecca looks past my shoulder and breaks out into a huge smile. “Look!”

I turn to see what she’s looking at, and my mouth falls open.

“Opal, hi.” There Champ is, looking incredibly handsome. He’s wearing a clean, pressed shirt and jeans with a sharp crease ironed in. I’ve never seen him look so polished.

"You made it! I'm so happy to see you!" I can't help gushing because I honestly didn't think he would come. I feel like a girl with a high school crush because my heart is beating so fast that I think it may explode.

"Yeah, well, I thought I'd better come down and see what all the hoo-ha is about this chili."

"This is my friend, Rebecca. She's competing with her grandfather's recipe. You should taste it."

Champ takes a cup of the chili and tastes it. "This is really good," he says. "Have you ever competed before?"

Rebecca shakes her head. "No, I'm doing this as a tribute to my grandfather. He passed last year and always talked about entering this competition but never got around to it."

Champ nods sympathetically. "Well, that's a damn shame. This is damn good chili. You've got my vote."

"Thanks, Champ," Rebecca says, her voice filled with emotion. "That means a lot."

I'm interrupted by a voice. "Hey, Sis. I thought I'd find you here." I cringe as I hear my older brother's voice.

Champ stiffens, and he turns.

"What the hell are you doing here?" Doyle moves to stand in front of Champ, and I know this is not going to end well.

"This is your brother?" Champ looks at Doyle with barely disguised fury.

My heart sinks. This is so not how I wanted Champ to learn who my brother is.

"How do you know my sister? And what the fuck are you doing talking to her?"

Surprise fills Champ's face as he looks between Doyle and me.

"I'm doing the books at Champ's Gym, Doyle."

"You're what?" Doyle looks at me like I fell, hit my head, and never recovered.

"My friend, Shelly, set me up with a job. I'm getting work experience credit as I study for my degree."

"Surely you could have found something else." Doyle grimaces as he looks at me, then turns his head to glare at Champ.

"You should have told me who your brother was, Opal. I'm disappointed in you." My heart falls. I was so excited when I saw Champ, but of course Doyle had to show up and ruin everything.

I know I should have told Champ about my brother, but I thought if I could wait a little longer, he could overlook it. Everyone in Raytown knows how much Champ and my brother hate each other. I was surprised that Champ *didn't* know who I was.

"You need to step away from my sister," Doyle warns, getting up in Champ's face. I watch Champ as he fists his hands, his body ready to fight. "You know you can't beat me. I've already beaten you once. I don't need to prove myself again," my brother taunts.

"Don't start that shit with me, Doyle," Champ warns, his voice rising. "You cheated in that fight and you know it."

"I did no such thing. You have an ego the size of this state and can't admit that I beat you fair and square."

"The fuck you did," Champs says, anger lacing his voice.

"Hey, now, you two," I yell, getting them both to look at me before this gets out of hand. "Stop it right now. I don't want to see either of you fighting."

"Well, look who got to be Miss Bossy," my brother teases me.

I breathe a small sigh of relief when his rigid body language eases a little. At least I've diffused the situation slightly, though I know this is far from over for them and for me.

"I'm not going to stand for this. Opal, I'll see you at the gym. We need to talk." Champ's eyes are filled with so much disappointment and fury that it makes my heart hurt.

I nod as Champ turns and stomps away.

"Why'd you have to go and do that, you idiot? Are you happy now?" I yell at my brother.

"You're the idiot if you're working for Champ. I mean, come on, this town isn't that small. You could have found something else."

"But that's where I wanted to work. And just because you don't like him doesn't mean I can't make up my own mind about him." I face off with my brother, standing my ground and ready to defend my choices. I think it must be a universal Brother Code that they always think no man is good enough for their sister.

Doyle narrows his eyes at me. "Is there something going on between you two?"

I open and close my mouth, my cheeks burning.

"He better not be touching you."

"And you better not be telling me how to live my life. You need to give me some space," I tell my brother.

"But?"

"No buts about it. I'll talk to you later."

I say goodbye to Rebecca and search for Champ, so I can explain and convince him not to hate me. But everywhere I look, I can't find him. I run into the dusty parking lot, but his truck is gone. "Dammit," I say, slapping my hand against my leg.

I don't know why those two have to go at each other like wild cats. But after growing up with three older brothers, I understand fragile male egos and how men hate backing down. The need to be right is programmed into their genetic code.

Champ has a huge amount of pride. I've heard about the fight between Doyle and Champ from my brother, and to hear him tell it, he beat Champ fair and square. But my brother is also a braggart, so who knows? What I do know is that there are always two sides to a story, and nothing is ever black and white. I also know it was years ago. Why they're still in a twist over this is stupid. Win or lose, it's something they should have gotten past by now.

I only hope Champ can forgive me for keeping this from him. I like the job and want to keep working at his gym. If he throws me out of the job, he'll probably never willingly see me again, and that hurts my heart in a whole different way. I can't bear to lose my shot with Champ.

CHAPTER 4

Monday mornings are never good mornings, especially today.

Everything was fine until I remembered Friday night and what happened with Opal and her brother. I've been stewing over it all weekend. Finding out that her brother is Doyle Malone was a sucker punch. I never even thought about that when I learned that they shared the last name because Malone's not uncommon around here. But fuck, she's related to that cheating son of a bitch. That asshole cheated in a fight, and it was my only loss in the ring.

Heading to the gym usually makes me happy, but today? My emotions are a mix of anger, frustration, and disappointment. I need to talk to Opal, but I'm apprehensive about how it will go. But we need to talk and I need to figure out the lay of the land and whether or not I can keep trusting her.

"Goddammit," I yell, pounding the heel of my hand against the wheel of my truck.

It hasn't stopped vibrating since I hit the freeway to head to Jefferson. Opal's there with Luann, who's training her on some fancy new software for the computer she made me buy. I don't know what's wrong with the hardcover account books I've been using for years, but Luann pitched a fit and said it was necessary.

I signal and pull over to the side of the road and call Rebel Autos. I know that whatever's happening, the truck isn't getting any better on its own. The last thing I need is it crapping out on me while I'm doing 70 on the freeway.

"Hey man," I say when Mack answers the phone.

"Champ, my man, how's it going?"

"Well, not so good, Mack. My truck is about to break down, and I'm stuck on the freeway. I'm on the road to Jefferson and my new gym. Can you send someone to tow me? I don't want my truck to stop in the middle of the road and cause a massive accident."

"Champ, man, we got you covered," Mack says. "I'll send one of the guys out right now. Should be about forty-five minutes."

"Got it. I'm on the freeway between markers thirty-five and thirty-six."

"Okay. You hang tight, and we'll get you."

I turn on my hazards and sit in the cab of my truck, trying and failing not to keep looping Friday night in my mind. It's been a long time since I felt an inkling of an attraction to a woman, and longer still since a woman asked me out, even though a chili cook-off isn't what most people would call a date. Every fiber of my being needs to see and talk to her, but

I have to do it in person. There are conversations you should not have on the phone, and this is one of them.

Finally, a tow truck pulls up in front of me, and I recognize Roman getting out. I check the traffic and then step out of my truck to meet him. "Roman, man. It's been a while, hasn't it? They got you driving the tow truck now?"

"Yeah, it's been too long, man. I go where I'm needed." He laughs. "Truth is, our regular guy is out with the flu, and I'm the only one with experience driving a tow truck." Roman hitches up my truck in short order, and we get on our way.

"You don't seem to come around Jefferson much anymore," Roman says as we head to Jefferson.

"Well, I've been coming around, but it's mostly to deal with the new gym. My hands have been full. Between that and helping Harley lately, I haven't had time for anything else. I'll be around more once the new gym is open, and I'll have more time to relax and see you guys."

"I've heard Harley's busy these days. It's a shame. It's always better when things are quiet for him because that means the world is a little bit safer."

"Yeah, Harley's the one keeping it safe. I think I'm going to be making a trip up to King Mountain soon with some supplies. I know he's stashed a couple of women up there for protection, and he had me pick up a load of supplies last week."

"Glad you're able to help him out, Champ. I know he appreciates how much he can rely on you."

"Thanks, man. I just do what I can. If someone's in need, you know I'll do whatever I can to help."

Roman nods. "Yeah, you've always been like that. You're a good man."

"Thanks," I say, ready to change the conversation. Roman's right that I like helping people, but I don't necessarily want to talk about it. I don't need people thanking me for what any decent human being should also be doing. "What's new with you, Roman? How's that girl of yours, Tessa?"

"Man," Roman says, rubbing a hand through his hair. "She's a handful. Fourteen years old and thinks she knows better than me about what she wants to do with her life."

"Uh oh," I chuckle. "What's been going on?"

"She's got it into her pretty little head that she wants to be a writer." Roman looks at me and arches his eyebrow like this is the most outlandish thing in the world.

"What's wrong with being a writer, Roman?"

"Well, I don't want her to be poor. You know it's a hard way for anyone to make money. I mean, how many writers make it?"

"I don't know, Roman, it's not my thing. My sister's the reader in our family."

"Yeah, I just… I want her to have a better life than I had, you know? Before I went into the Army, things were tough. I would've ended up in prison if it weren't for the Army. You know that."

"Yeah, man. I think it was like that for a lot of guys. The army saved us."

"Yeah, but Tessa, she's not... interested in going into the army or any other branch. What's worse, I think one of her teachers at the high school is encouraging this." Roman drives down the off-ramp into Jefferson and heads toward Rebel Autos.

"Are you dating anyone, Roman?"

"No," Roman says, shaking his head. "Sometimes I wish I was, but you know I've got rules."

I chuckle. Roman has always had rules for everything, but some of his rules kept us alive when we were serving in Iraq. You got to give the man some credit.

"The girl needs the influence of a woman in her life, but I've told her she can't date until she's eighteen—and part of the deal is that I won't date either."

I look at Roman in shock. He was never one to be without a woman for long. "Man, how are you going to get a female influence in her life if you don't have one in yours?"

"That's the conundrum, Champ. You know I lead by example."

"You're committed to her, aren't you?"

"I am, yeah. I'm gonna make sure she has the best start in the world. It was a shock to come home and find out I had a daughter and another shock when my ex said it was 'my turn' and then took off. If I have to deny myself some things to give her the best start in life, it's worth it."

"Have you ever considered that the rules are holding you back?"

Roman looks at me with exasperation, like he expected me to agree with him automatically.

"Do you want me to fix your truck or what?" He mock-challenges me but eventually laughs.

"Okay, man, I take it back." I laugh. "But think about it. It could be a good influence for both of you."

"You think my daughter dating will be a good influence on her?"

"Roman, I don't know what to say, but don't you remember what it was like to be fourteen? Don't you miss having a woman in your life?"

Roman looks at me and grudgingly nods. "We should talk about something else. What are you coming out here to Jefferson for? Checking on the new gym?"

"Yeah, partly," I say. "I might have an issue with my bookkeeper, so I came here to talk to her. I saw her Friday night, and it didn't go well."

"Really?" Roman asks.

"Yeah, you'll never guess who her goddamn brother is."

Roman glances at me as if to say, "Go on."

"Her brother is motherfucking Doyle Malone."

"No shit. Wait a minute. This is his sister, his twin?"

"Apparently so," I say. "She doesn't look a goddamn bit like him, which is good because he's an ugly son of a bitch. I would never have hired her, even with Shelly's recommendation."

"Yeah, I don't envy you that situation. What are you going to do?"

"Honestly, I don't know. I need to talk to her and see how I feel after that. I need her to run the books at the gym, and she helps keep an eye on things. But if I can't trust her..."

"Yeah, I know what you mean. Good luck with that."

"Thanks, I think I'm going to need it. Speaking of, can you drop me off at the gym?" I ask. Rebel Autos isn't that far from the gym, but I want to get this over sooner than I could if I had to walk over there.

"Sounds good, man. I'll call when I have an update on your truck."

Roman drops me off and I take a deep breath. This might not go well.

CHAPTER 5

I close the door to the office and turn off the computer screen.

"Why'd you do that, Opal?" Shelly asks.

"I need to talk. I think I've blown it with Champ."

"Uh oh," Shelly says. "We need to get Beth in on this conversation. Boot the computer back up."

I pull up the video conference software and call Beth. All the while, I'm looking through the office window to keep an eye out if Champ shows up.

Beth says, "Hey, ladies! What's up? How did it go Friday night?" Beth leans forward, clearly excited.

I wince at the memory. "Champ showed up."

"Girl, so what's the problem?" Shelly asks, turning to me.

"The problem is right after he showed up, so did my brother. They got into it, and Champ stormed off."

"Uh oh," Shelly repeats. "Have you talked to him since?"

"No, but I called the gym in Raytown for something, and he wasn't there. I'm scared he's on his way here, and he's going to fire me."

Shelly shakes her head. "He needs you too much in this office. I set it up, but it can't run without somebody there, and I can't do both offices. Besides, you live here in Jefferson, so it makes sense for you to work here."

"I know, but..." Tears prick my eyes. "I feel so terrible for letting him down. I can't describe the look of disappointment in his eyes. He looked so betrayed."

"He probably does feel that way," Beth says. "You know how much he hates your brother. Champ generally lets things go, but he's still sore over the fight he lost to Doyle. He goes around telling everybody how Doyle cheated."

"That's not how my brother tells it," I say, rolling my eyes.

"Yeah, with these two, who knows what's true," Beth says. "But the point is, the cat's out of the bag, and now you've got to deal with it."

"Do you have any suggestions on what I should say?" I ask, feeling desperate.

"Just be honest. You didn't want to tell him because you knew how he would react, and you wanted him to give you a chance, not dismiss you because of who your brother is."

"She's got a good point, Opal," Shelly says, agreeing with Beth. "Don't try to hide anything."

"I don't think there's anything left to hide." I sigh. "Oh, God." Tension ripples across my skin. "He's here. I'll talk to you guys later."

“Good luck,” they say in unison.

I end the video conference and close the software. I don't want to give Champ any more reason to be mad at me.

“I'm going to take this as my cue to leave,” Shelly says, hugging me. “Hang in there, and don't let him steamroll you. Call me later.”

“Thanks, Shelly. I will.”

“You're leaving?” Champ asks, looking confused.

“Yeah, I'm all finished up. Opal's doing great with the software, so I'm letting her do some work and get used to it. I'll see you back in Raytown.”

“See you later,” Champ says, his eyebrow arched at Shelly's swift departure.

Champ stands in the doorway of the office and turns to face me.

“Hi, Champ. I'm—”

“What the hell happened at the Chili cook-off, Opal?” Champ cuts me off. “How come you didn't tell me your brother is Doyle Malone?”

“Hello to you too,” I say, trying to compose myself under his fierce glare. “I didn't tell you because I was pretty sure this is exactly what would happen. I've heard how my brother talks about you, and it's probably the same way you talk about him. Growing up with three brothers and seeing their stubbornness about rivalries, I knew you would be blinded by it. Would you have given me a chance if you knew he was my brother?”

Champ looks at me for a long moment and shakes his head. "I sure as hell wouldn't."

"See, that's exactly it. You want to judge me for something my brother did or didn't do years ago."

"He most certainly *did* cheat in that fight," Champ says hotly.

I hold up my hands. There's no way my brother or Champ are being one hundred percent honest about what happened, and I'm not interested in hearing either try to justify why they're right, and the other is wrong. "Regardless of what happened in that fight, it has nothing to do with me. You should also know that I love my brother, even if he is a pain in the ass sometimes. Do you understand that, Champ?"

"Yeah, I can understand that, Opal," he concedes, his voice evening out. "You have to understand that honesty is the most important thing to me. Is there anything else you're withholding from me?"

"Absolutely not," I say without hesitation. "I'm exactly the person you think I am. I'm a woman who took a while to figure out what I wanted in life, and now I'm a college student who loves working for you. Champ, I'm sorry I didn't tell you who my brother is. Are we going to be okay? Or did you come here to fire me?"

Champ inhales deeply and crosses his arms over his muscular chest. "Aside from talking to you, I wasn't sure what I was coming here to do. I can't deny that firing you crossed my mind several times. But you do a good job, and I like having you around."

Even though this is a serious conversation, my heart skips a beat. "You like having me around?"

"Don't read too much into it," he says, his voice gruff again, but the air between us feels clearer and more positive. "You can stay, but if you ever hold anything back from me again, we're gonna have a very different conversation."

"I understand, Champ. I won't keep anything from you. I promise on everything."

"Good. Shelly says you're getting on okay with the software?"

"Yeah, it's fine. It's not too different from what we used in one of my classes at the college. Once you figure out the menus, it's all straightforward."

Champ nods and pauses for a moment as he looks at me. It takes all my nerve to maintain eye contact with him. It's important that he sees me as a strong woman, even if I feel like a quivering mess inside.

"Good. I'm glad to hear that. Oh, hey, I've got to take this call," Champ says as he takes a ringing phone out of his pocket.

"Hey, Roman, what's up?" I hear Champ say. "Fuck man, seriously? Okay, thanks for letting me know. No, no, don't worry about it. I'll figure out a way to get back to Raytown."

"Is everything okay?" I ask after Champ ends his phone call.

"No. Goddamn truck broke down on my way here. I need a new engine block, and I'm not going to have my truck for at least a week."

"Oh, man, that sucks. Is there anything I can help you with?"

"No, no. I'll be fine," he grumbles. "Goddammit, why is my phone ringing again? Oh, hey, Harley. I'll be back in a minute." Champ pauses for a moment and leaves the office, walking to the other side of the gym.

I watch him outside the gym office. His expression is more serious than I've ever seen, like he's preparing for bad news. I see him nod a couple of times and make a face. "Yeah, okay, Harley. I don't have my truck, but I'll figure it out. I'll get you everything today."

"Is there something I can help you with?" I ask when Champ comes back to the office.

Champ looks at me assessingly. "Are you finished up here for the day or close enough to it?"

"Yeah, I have some more invoices to enter, but they're nothing urgent." Champ looks at me as if deciding whether he can trust me and if he wants to admit he needs help.

"What kind of car do you got?"

"I've got an SUV."

"Okay, that'll work. I need to take some supplies to my buddy Harley up on King Mountain. Are you up for that?"

"Sure, yeah. Whatever you need, I can help."

"We might need to stay overnight because it's a bit of a drive. Is that okay?"

A thousand thoughts race through my mind. An overnight trip with Champ? Hell, yeah. This may not be how I expected to spend time with Champ, but there's no way I'm going to say no to spending several hours and possibly staying overnight on King Mountain with him.

"Yeah, I just need to pick up a change of clothes at home. I can spend the night up on the mountain if it comes to that," I say, mentally crossing my fingers that it turns out that way.

“Okay, good,” Champ says, some of the tension fading from his face. “Let’s get going.”

CHAPTER 6

"You're a good driver."

"You mean for a girl," Opal says, laughing easily. "My brothers taught me."

"I'm not used to being a passenger," I admit. "I don't know the last time someone drove me someplace."

Opal is silent for a moment as she passes a truck on the freeway, then glances at me. "It seems you do a lot of taking care of other people. Maybe let people in so they can take care of you, too?"

Opal's comment takes me by surprise. There's no teasing or malice to her statement. It's not like we've seen each other that much because Opal did most of her training in Jefferson. Yet she seems to see through to the person I am, not the gruff exterior that everyone else sees.

"Mm, possibly. One day." I look out the window of her SUV, enjoying the sight of the changing leaves. Before she can say anything else, I steer the conversation in another direction.

"So tell me about yourself. I know you're in college, and I know it must be awful to have the twin you do." I chuckle. "But tell me more about you."

"I'm not sure what there is to tell," Opal says, though her cheeks flush with heat. "What do you want to know?"

"What drives you? What do you want to do when you get out of college?"

"I want to work helping the community. You know that Doyle is a firefighter, and my other brothers are, too. We believe in giving back. I'd love to work with Warrior Cares. It would be great to help them expand the reach of their programs, so they can help more veterans. I believe in supporting the community and those who need help in supporting themselves. Warrior Cares is only a local organization now, but what if they could make it regional? Or national? It would be an honor to help them do that."

Of all the things she could've said, I'm both surprised and not surprised that this was her response. "That's impressive. I know a couple of people at Warrior Cares. I can put in a word for you if you like."

"I'd appreciate that!" Opal's smile is instant and bright. "Beth has introduced me to Antonia and Colleen. They host fundraisers for Warrior Cares, but they don't work for them. Any introduction helps, you know?"

"Of course. I'm happy to help, though that leaves me in the position of finding another person to help in the office." I suppress a sigh. Sometimes I wish I didn't have to deal with the business side of running a business, but I'm the first to admit that I don't like giving control or access to other people, especially strangers.

“I’m sure Shelly or I could help you with that when the time comes.”

Realizing how much I’d miss Opal if she left catches me off guard. She’ll mostly be working in the Jefferson gym when it opens soon, but the idea that I wouldn’t see her at all makes me rethink my promise to help her find a different job.

A comfortable silence falls between us as Opal drives on. Dusk is starting to fill the sky when we take the turnoff to reach the two-lane road that will take us up to King Mountain.

“Champ,” Opal says, glancing at me, “I need you to be straight with me.”

“What’s your question?” I ask, uneasy. It’s never a good sign when a woman asks you to be straight with her.

“Are you going to give me an honest answer?” she persists, gripping the steering wheel tighter.

“It depends on what you’re going to ask me.” I’m not in the habit of lying, but I am in the habit of being private. People spend far too much time these days sharing things that should be kept private.

“Alright. Does this trip and all the stuff in the back,” she jerks her head to the bags piled up in her backseat, “have anything to do with the cash withdrawals you won’t explain?”

I take a deep breath. When I asked her for help today, I knew explaining everything to her was unavoidable. To my surprise, I’m not hesitant to do so. “Yes, it does.”

“Champ,” she says, a hint of exasperation in her voice. “Will you tell me, or are you going to make me grill you?”

"Sorry. I'm not used to talking about this, so I don't know where to start."

"Okay. How about explaining what all these bags are about?"

"Right. Those are supplies for women."

Opal turns to me and raises an eyebrow.

"You've probably heard me talk about my buddy Harley."

"Yes, I've heard his name. I don't know who he is to you, though."

"We go back a long way. To make that long story short, he, and now his wife, help to fight human trafficking. Mostly, he sends money to people in other countries to prevent these women from ending up here or in another country. But he also works to rescue those women if they do end up here." I pause to look at Opal. She nods, but her jaw is clenched. "These bags are for some women he rescued this week."

Opal pauses as she takes this in. "So why are they up on King Mountain?"

"We have some buddies up there. Waylon and his men own a bunch of property. Well, they own half the damn mountain. Some of it they run as a business. They have vacation cabins they rent and cabins they use to hide people until it's safe for them to go home or find a new place to call home."

Opal keeps driving, her fingers wrapping and rewrapping around the steering wheel. "Is this where the money from the cash withdrawals goes?"

"Some of it, yes," I say simply. "Some of the money is for supplies like we're bringing. Most of it goes directly to Harley. There's a lot of bribery and payoffs involved in working to shut down these operations, whether it's here or in the countries these women are taken from."

"How did you get involved in this?"

I inhale and wait as Opal navigates a busy intersection. "We met through mutual friends. He's an unaffiliated biker. He used to belong to a club, but he struck out on his own. When he first told me about what he does, I thought about what I would do if something like this happened to Beth, and I was immediately on board. These women and their families don't deserve this kind of cruelty," I tell her, unable to keep the passion out of my voice. "We give money and supplies; people like Waylon and his crew offer safe shelter and protection. Harley is a loner, but he's built a rock-solid network. He's been at this a while. This works on absolute trust and secrecy." I look at Opal, making sure she understands. "That means you can't talk about any of this, not even to Beth or Shelly."

"I understand. Beth and Shelly know about this?" Opal asks, clearly surprised.

"No, they don't, and they don't need to." I emphasize my words. It's no secret women love to gossip, but I'm taking a chance with Opal. I'm confident she can keep her mouth shut, but I still feel the need to drive home the importance of the secrecy of this.

"If this is so secret, how come you're letting me come up here with you?"

I take a deep breath. "Well, the damn truck crapped out on me, for one. More than that, I know what you went through trying to help your sister. We don't know each other well – yet—but I know someone like you understands this more than the average person. You don't seem quite as much of a gossip as my sister or other women."

"Thanks, I guess?" Opal says, but her joyful laugh fills the car. "But wait. How did Beth and Shelly deal with the cash withdrawals? They've both worked on your books."

At this, I chuckle. "They classified them as something. I'm stubborn, and they didn't need to know."

"Shocking!" Opal's voice is teasing, and it makes me smile. More seriously, she adds, "I understand about keeping this private. You can rely on me."

"That's what I'm counting on." I reach out and touch her arm, and she turns to me and smiles.

Fuck. I want to see that smile for a long time to come.

"Take a left at the fork. We're here."

CHAPTER 7

"I admire what you're doing, Champ. This isn't something I would have guessed. Not that I think you don't care about people," I add quickly. "More like you've kept this so quiet. Everyone knows how much community means to you and how much you give."

"Thanks, Opal. I know what you meant. Just pull into the parking here, and we'll hike the rest of the way. It's not far."

I pull my scarf tightly around my throat to ward off the chill of the mountain air. Everything up here is crisp and cold, and it's barely sunset. Champ hands me a couple of bags, then carries most of them himself.

He leads me to a cabin with lights blazing. He knocks loudly on the door, and a voice calls out, telling us the door is open. Inside the cabin, a fire is blazing, and a burly, bearded man stands in front of a beeping microwave.

"Champ! Good to see you!" The man puts a steaming mug of coffee on the counter and comes over to slap Champ on the shoulder.

"Good to see you, too, Waylon. Though I wish the circumstances were better."

Waylon nods. "You know the door is always open for you. But you need to actually come up to visit and take the offer," Waylon says, making it sound like this is a longstanding exchange between them.

"Yeah, I know. I'll work on it. This is Opal." Champ gestures toward me. "She's one of the ladies helping me run the office side of things at the gyms."

"That's right. I heard you were opening a second location."

"Yeah, I am. The Jefferson location will be open soon. A woman came in for a self-defense class with one of my guys. She knocked out her ex, and someone caught it on video and posted it online. Damn video went viral, so now I have a waitlist for both gyms, and women want self-defense classes."

Champ makes it sound like it's a burden, but he can't help smiling a little at the demand for the new gym, not to mention helping more women with self-defense classes.

"That's good work, Champ. You should be proud."

"I am. But I couldn't do it without help," he says, turning to me. "I need Opal and Shelly to help me with the books and keep it all straight. It's a small wonder I kept the first gym running as long as I did on my own."

Champ and Waylon look at me, and my cheeks flush with pride.

"Oh, I don't do that much," I say.

"The hell you don't. I know everyone thinks I'm a mean bastard, but don't ever doubt how much I value and appreciate you, Opal. I'm serious." Champ looks at me with an intensity that takes my breath away and makes my core twist with raw desire.

"Thank you." So many emotions roll through me, but I don't know what to say without making a fool of myself.

"I heard we had visitors. Champ, it's good to see you!" I have to make sure my mouth doesn't hang open as I watch a woman with dark brown hair pulled back in a ponytail go up to Champ and hug him. Jealousy flares until I see a ring on her left hand.

"Opal, come and meet Claudia. She and Glen live here on the mountain, running a dog shelter. They work with Warrior Cares."

As I shake the woman's hand, it clicks into place. "Oh! Do you mean Sweet Redemption Refuge? I've heard about that!"

"Yeah, that's us. I'm Glen." A man with haunted eyes smiles and extends his hand to me. "That's how we met. I adopted a rescue dog…"

"Mutt." Claudia smiles, wrapping her arms around his torso.

"Yeah. That little SOB—pardon my language—wasn't behaving. The shelter I adopted him from recommended training classes with this woman, and now we're out here. Much quieter than back in the city," he says, his eyes creasing with stress.

"It sounds like you have your hands full." I watch as Champ talks to a man who's just walked into the cabin. "Is this place…like an office?"

"Something like that. Waylon lives here, but it's where everyone comes to meet, and this is the official-unofficial," Claudia makes air quotes, "office for this side of the mountain. There are some cabins rented out and…other business. This serves as the office for everything. Everyone reports to Waylon."

"Champ told me about the women being helped," I say. It's obvious she's intentionally being vague, which makes sense given what Champ described to me on the way here.

Claudia nods and relaxes a little. "I'm impressed that Champ told you. It was shocking to see that he brought someone up here, to be honest. He's never done that before."

"Well, his truck is in the shop. He asked, and it sounded urgent, so I couldn't say no."

"Hm. He could have rented or borrowed a car." Claudia gives me a long look like she's sizing me up. "Is there anything else? Are you two dating?"

I glance away, my cheeks burning with a blush. It doesn't seem like it should be so obvious, but Claudia's right – he could have asked someone else or rented a truck. I'm realizing that Champ allowing me to join him on this trip is a really big deal.

"No. I mean, it's not that I don't want it, but he always keeps me at arm's distance. I asked him out, but then my brother showed up – and they hate each other. That went as well as you'd expect," I sigh. "I'm not sure if anything is going to happen." As I say the words, I begin to question them. Why would Champ ask me to drive him today if he wanted to keep me at a distance? Maybe he likes me more than he lets on?

Claudia smiles. "By the way he keeps glancing at you, I'd say you have a chance. He's not letting you out of his sight."

I look over my shoulder and smile when Champ meets my gaze. A shiver of desire dances over my skin.

"You two should stay for dinner. There's always room up here," Claudia offers.

"It is getting late," I say, looking out the window at the darkening sky, then glancing over to where Champ's standing and talking to Waylon.

"Nonsense. There are empty cabins up here, too." Claudia winks at me, and it feels like another person is trying to set me up with Champ.

"What are you two ladies talking about over here?" Champ joins us, and I hold my breath.

"I was telling Opal that you two should stay for dinner. I've made a pan of lasagna, and there's plenty to share. Why don't you spend the night up here?"

I freeze, part of me silently cursing Claudia for saying this but also thanking her.

Champ pauses and looks at me, his eyes intense. "That sounds good to me. Opal, what do you think?"

I look at Champ and nod. He mentioned we might have to spend the night up here, but I didn't think it would actually happen.

"Perfect!" Claudia exclaims, clapping her hands.

I can't help but smile at how it feels like everyone is trying to set us up together. At least tonight, there's precisely zero chance my brother will show up and ruin things.

CHAPTER 8

Opal is dealing with everything and everyone up here better than I could have imagined. It's not too surprising, given how she shares a commitment to helping people, but it's reassuring. This would be a lot for most people to take in over a short period of time. Knowing that Opal understands and respects my commitment to these people is deeply important to me.

Even though she's sitting next to me at the dinner table, she gets skittish every time we make eye contact.

"How you doing over there?" I ask quietly, reaching out and touching her arm.

Opal glances at my hand on her arm, but she doesn't flinch. Lifting her eyes to mine, she smiles.

"It's a lot to take in. This isn't what I expected when you said you needed to help someone on the mountain."

"What did you think I meant?" I ask, genuinely curious.

"I'm not sure." She pauses. "But not this. How come you don't talk about it?"

I lean back in my chair and look at Opal. Being with her feels natural. I like that I don't have to hide any part of who I am. Talking about myself and my motivations to others isn't something I do—or want to do—but I want Opal to see me. My feelings for her are growing, but I need to know she's on board with all this and who I am. I don't want her to be a part of my life; I need her to be a part of my life.

"I don't feel the need to make a big deal about it. Besides, part of why the network works is because we keep quiet about it. As you can imagine, some people are violently opposed to us interfering with their plans. The safety of these women is at serious risk if word gets out about what we do."

"Sure." Opal nods. "But you could get more people to help."

"Well, I have you now." My voice is low, but the way her blue eyes flare slightly, I know she heard and picked up on what I mean. "I don't do this for awards or to impress other people. I do it because it's the right thing to do. There's a way for me to help, so I do. That's it."

"It's more than that, and you know it, Champ. You're helping to save these women's lives." Opal's eyes have a fierce intensity as she looks at me.

"Yes. And now that Shelly is part of the gym, it's a little more personal. She wasn't trafficked, but she was abused just the same. I have no tolerance for people, especially men, who prey on other people."

"I appreciate that you trust me, Champ. Though I will say that I wasn't sure how things would work out after what happened at the chili cook-off. I was sure you were going to fire me, and that would be the end of everything."

I lean toward Opal because she needs to know how serious I am. "I don't want you to leave, Opal. I don't want you to leave, ever. Stay with me." My voice is heavy with longing. If Opal still has any doubts that I believe in her and want her around, I need to eliminate them.

A bright happiness lights up Opal's eyes, and she blushes prettily. "So you're okay with everything? Okay with who my brother is?"

"Opal, I'm never going to like your brother. But with you at the gym and in my life, I swear I'll try to be civil to the man. You're important to me."

Opal's blush deepens, and I shift in my chair as my cock tightens and pulsates with desire.

"You're important to me, too," she says, her voice quiet.

I take her hand, lightly stroking her wrist with my thumb. "I like having you around. I want to continue that."

"Yes," she says immediately, putting her hand over mine. "I'd love that. I should add that I still want to work for Warrior Cares, but I know that's unlikely to happen until I graduate."

"There's still time between now and then," I say. "Maybe I'll convince you to stay at the gym."

Opal's voice is teasing as she smiles at me. "Oh, really?"

"Yes, really," I say, my voice low. Seeing Opal playful makes my body surge with need for her. She has curves I want to mold against my body, whether I'm making love to her or we're curled up watching TV at the end of the day. Her body is fucking gorgeous. "Why don't we head up to the cabin? I'll grab a bottle of whiskey, and we can sit on the porch."

"I'm all yours."

* * *

THE SUN SETS over the mountains, painting the sky in oranges and pinks. I grab two glasses and head out to the cabin porch, where Opal is curled up in a chair with a blanket over her lap. Sitting beside Opal, I pour two fingers of whiskey into each glass and hand one to her.

She takes a sip, and I see the appreciation in her eyes as the whiskey slides down her throat.

"This is good," she says appreciatively.

I nod. "I'm glad you like it."

Opal smiles at me, her blue eyes shining in the fading light. I take a deep breath and enjoy the peaceful moment. She looks so beautiful. We sip our drinks in silence, the sun ebbing away and the stars emerging in the night sky.

Opal turns to me, and our eyes meet. I can tell that she wants to say something, but she hesitates.

"What is it?" I ask, my voice low and gentle.

She takes a deep breath and then meets my gaze. "I have a confession to make."

Anticipation builds inside me as I wait for her to continue.

"I… I have a crush on you," she finally blurts out. Her skin is flushed from the whiskey, but I know she's not drunk.

My heart pounds in my chest, and desire courses through my body. I suspected she felt this way but hearing her confirm it makes all the difference in the world.

I reach out and take her hand in mine. "I have a confession to make, too," I whisper, my voice filled with desire. "I've noticed. I'm attracted to you, too."

Opal's eyes widen with surprise before filling with a warm, happy light. "That's not what I thought you'd say." She smiles, taking another sip of her whiskey.

"Why not?" I ask, curious.

"Because you always stay away from me when you see me at the gym."

"Opal," I say, looking into her eyes. "It's not because I don't like you—it's because I've wanted you so damn much, but there are little things like laws about making a pass at your bookkeeper—no matter how sexy they look in a dress."

"You don't know how happy that makes me, Champ. I wasn't sure you noticed me in those dresses." Opal's bright eyes meet mine, and I know what happens between us tonight will change everything.

I have no hesitation when it comes to Opal. We have a long way to go to know each other better, but I know we will, as much as I know my heart is right for wanting her. I welcome our future with open arms.

"A blind man would appreciate you in those dresses, Opal. I think we should have a toast," I say, raising my glass. The sun is almost gone now, but the fire in my heart burns brighter.

"To what?" she asks, her blue eyes searching mine.

"To us," I say. "To what could be."

"I'll drink to that." Opal's smile punches me in the heart with how happy it makes me. We both take long sips from our glasses, our eyes never breaking as we drink.

"Opal," I murmur, my voice quiet as the light fades and the sounds of the forest surround us. "Will you let me kiss you?"

For a moment, her eyes search mine, then her face breaks into a beautiful smile, and she nods.

My heart soars with joy as I stand and pull her to me, pressing my lips gently against hers. We share a tender kiss. Her heart beats wildly against my chest, racing just as fast as my heart.

The kiss deepens as our tongues move faster, building our passion. Her body presses hard against mine, showing me that she feels the same desire that I do.

My hands slip around her waist, and I pull her tighter, relishing the sensation of her moaning into our kiss. I love that she's sharing herself with me like this. We finally break the kiss, and the hunger in her eyes is naked and bright. Her soft lips linger on mine, the heat of her skin radiating through my body. Electricity runs between us.

"I want to make love to you tonight," I whisper, my voice low and urgent.

I slowly move my hands up her arms, and she trembles as I stroke her skin. There's no denying the fire of our desire tonight.

Opal reaches up, runs her hand along my jaw, then pulls my head to hers and kisses me again. "Then take me, Champ."

CHAPTER 9

My fingers trace the outline of his abs, feeling the defined ridges and valleys of his muscles. I can't believe this is happening, that he's here with me, inviting me into his life and his bed.

Unable to resist any longer, I slide to my knees in front of Champ and take him into my mouth. He grows harder and tangles his hands in my hair as I work my mouth over him, swirling my tongue around the sensitive tip before taking him deep into my throat.

His body tenses beneath me, his breath coming in short gasps as my tongue lavishes attention on his long cock. As he starts moaning, I quicken my pace and use my hand to stroke him as I take him deeper into my mouth.

Champ's body tenses beneath me, his breathing jagged as his fingers tug my hair and guide my head. A powerful heat builds inside me, begging to be released, but I want Champ to feel how much I long for him. I lose myself as I quicken my pace, focusing on Champ's hard cock.

Champ's body shakes as he grips my hair, but he suddenly pulls away from me, gasping for breath. "Opal, stop."

A swirl of anxiety and embarrassment rises in my chest. "What did I do?" I ask, my voice barely a whisper as I nervously look away from him. Have I completely misunderstood the situation?

Champ gently cups my chin and lifts my face to his. His dark eyes search mine, a look of fierce tenderness in them. "Opal, sweetheart. You've done nothing wrong." His voice is soft and reassuring as he continues, "I want to be inside you when I come, and I want us to come together. My cock needs to be buried in you."

My heart skips a beat as I breathe a sigh of relief. Champ pulls me closer, his lips finding mine in a passionate kiss that leaves me breathless. He runs his hands over my body as his mouth claims mine again, setting my skin on fire with desire. We laugh as we fall into bed, our hands never leaving each other.

His fingers trail down my breasts and stomach before slipping between my legs and pressing against the slick heat of my desire. I moan and push myself against his fingers as they move in circles around my core.

Champ moves his body over mine, and I arch my hips to meet him, eager to have him inside me. He kisses me deeply, his tongue tangling with mine as he enters me with a slow, strong stroke, stretching me in the most delicious way. I gasp as I give myself over to pleasure, my hands gripping his shoulders as he begins to move inside me.

Each thrust is slow and deep, filling me completely as he rocks his hips against mine. I wrap my legs around him, pulling him closer as we move together. I'm lost in ecstasy as we hold each other tightly, moving faster and faster as our bodies take over and we let go.

Champ's thrusts become rougher and more intense, making my body sing from exhilaration and love. An intensity is building within me, and my body bucks against him. My orgasm is so close, and my muscles are taut with the need to come.

I wrap my arms around his back, holding Champ tightly against my body as he thrusts into me harder and faster, his breathing jagged.

"God, Opal, you feel so fucking amazing," Champ grunts, his voice thick with desire. He looks into my eyes, and our connection pushes me over the edge.

I cry out as my walls clench around Champ's cock, and my orgasm crashes through me in waves. I hold him, matching the rhythm of his thrusts until he loses control and yells my name as he comes.

Champ and I lie in bed breathless as we face each other, sharing lingering touches. His body quivers with the after-shocks of his orgasm as we catch our breath, both blissfully sated. His heart beats against my chest as he nuzzles his face into my neck, his warm breath tickling my skin.

"I love you, Opal." His voice is husky and raw with emotion. "I know this is fast, but I know how I feel about you. With you, I have no doubt."

I stroke his hair gently and lean in to kiss him tenderly, tears of joy pricking at the corners of my eyes. "I love you too, Champ. I knew when I first saw you that you were special, and I was attracted to you. You are more than I imagined, and I love every bit of you."

Champ pulls me against his chest and hugs me fiercely. "Even if I don't love your brother?"

I laugh and playfully swat at his arm. "We can work on that. You said you would."

I take her hand in mine. "As you know, I am a man of my word. I make no promises, but," he smiles as he leans his head to mine and gives me a long kiss, "I promise on my life that I'll do my best."

"Good." I smile as I kiss him back. For both of us, family means everything, and he knows how much my brother means to me.

Our kiss deepens, and my heart expands with our love and joy. Calling Champ mine has always been a wild dream. Now that it's a reality, I know that how I reacted to him when I first met him was my soul finding its forever mate.

And now, it's time for us to create a life of our own. Together forever.

EPILOGUE

"Again, thank you all for coming here today and for welcoming Champ's Gym to Jefferson. I look forward to meeting everyone and working with a new group of boxers here. We are committed to community, which means that self-defense classes for women and our new program for teens will remain free of charge."

The crowd claps as Champ finishes his speech. My heart swells with so much love for him as he formally opens the doors to the new gym to let people come in and have a look. He has put so much effort into making sure that the new location of the gym will serve the community and not just boxers.

"You were wonderful, Champ," I say, giving him a kiss and a big hug.

He hugs me back and smiles. "I'll be spending a lot of time at this location, I'll have you know."

He winks at me and I grin back at him. I lace my fingers through his and hold his hand as we watch the crowd.

I know he's going to be here to get the new gym up and running. He's already been spending so much time at my place that I've already given him a few drawers of my dresser for all of his things.

"As much as I'd love to stay here with you, my dear Opal, I need to go talk to the crowd first."

"Go and do your thing," I tell him, squeezing his hand. "I totally understand. I'll be here for you when you're back."

I look at the crowd, pleased that so many people have shown up for the opening today. I even saw my brothers, which makes me happy. Doyle still isn't quite on board with me being involved with Champ. But I've told him that Champ is my boyfriend and he better get used to it. We all had an awkward dinner a couple of weeks ago, but we made it through without any fistfights or yelling. I consider that a win.

I pull my jacket around me and walk over to where Beth and Dirk are standing under a tree.

"Hey, you two," I say, pulling Beth into a hug. "How are you guys doing?"

"We're doing great, thanks," Dirk says. "But Beth here has some news."

"Are you sure, Dirk?" she asks, looking at him, uncertainty and excitement in her eyes.

"Maybe we should get your brother over here too."

When Beth nods, Dirk makes his way to where Champ is standing and talking with a few people.

I raise my eyebrow at Beth. "What's the secret?"

"I'll tell you now, but you have to act surprised when Dirk comes back and we tell my brother. Champ will be mad if he thinks that he wasn't the first to know." She giggles and threads her arm through mine.

"Okay," I say. "What's going on?"

Beth smiles, and her whole face glows with happiness. She puts her hand to her stomach and looks down.

"Oh, my god! Do you mean…?" I ask, my voice raising a couple of octaves.

"I do," she exclaims. "We're having a baby!"

"I'm so happy for you, Beth. You and Dirk are going to be amazing parents." I wrap my arms around Beth and hug her tightly, bursting with happiness for her.

"I'm really excited but also terrified. Everything is so perfect with our life that this almost seems like too much perfection."

"Enjoy it," I tell her. "You deserve all the happiness and I am so thrilled that everything is going so well for you two."

"Oh, here they come. Prepare to act surprised." She giggles.

"What's going on, sis? Dirk came over and grabbed me and said it was urgent that I come over and talk with you."

"Well," she says, "we have some news. I'm pregnant!"

As instructed, I squeal with happiness all over again while Champ shakes Dirk's hand and pulls him into a hug. I hear him muttering something to Dirk that sounds a lot like, "You better take good care of her or you'll answer to me."

"I heard that, Champ," Beth admonishes. "He'll answer to me and you know it."

"If you say so," Champ says, but he laughs. He pulls Beth into his arms and I can see his eyes glisten with tears that I know he won't let fall.

"I'm really happy for you, Beth. Anything you need, anything at all. And it's yours. The same for you, Dirk. You're family. And whatever you need, I'll make sure you have it."

"I appreciate that, man," Dirk says, wrapping his arm around Beth and holding her tightly.

He looks at Beth with such fierce love and devotion I can't help but sigh. It's exactly the way I feel when Champ looks at me.

"I guess this is as good a time as any," Champ says. "Dirk, I'm going to be spending a lot more time at the Jefferson Gym, which I know is no surprise to you. I want to invite you to take the lead at the Raytown gym while I'm here. I want you to look after all of the boys, lead the classes, and manage the place. Do you think you're up for that?"

"Are you serious?" Dirk says. "I would love that, Champ. Thank you for putting your trust in me."

"You're welcome, Dirk. You've earned it. I know I can trust you and that you won't let me down."

"I thought I'd find you here," Roman says, coming up behind Champ.

"Roman, hey, glad you made it. You want to sign up for some classes?" Champ jokes and slaps him on the shoulder.

"Nah, you know me. I'm not a boxer. I'm happy with my job at Rebel Autos and raising Tessa here," he says, looking at his daughter.

“Hey, Tessa, how are you?” I ask. I've only met her a couple of times, but she's a bright girl for her age.

“I'm doing okay, thanks,” she says, though I can see that something is troubling her.

When Roman, Dirk, and Champ go off to talk among themselves, and Beth goes to talk to another friend, I pull Tessa aside.

“Is everything okay?” I ask. “Are you having problems with school?”

“No, it's not school,” she says, still sulking. “Dad's just being a hardass.”

I raise my eyebrow at her cursing.

“Sorry,” she says. “Dad's being...he's being mean.”

“What's going on?”

“I want to study writing, but he keeps on telling me that I have to take all of these other academic classes. And that anything that I want to study has to be extracurricular. That wanting to do something creative isn't something he thinks I can be successful at. He's trying to block me from even trying.”

Tessa’s words come out in a hot rush and it’s obvious this has been eating at her. I know better than to try and parent another person's child, but I also know that kids need encouragement.

“Tessa, I know he has your best interest at heart,” I say. “I've only met him a few times. But I know he's very protective and devoted to you.

"I know," she says, barely concealing how she rolls her eyes. "I just wish that he would be more supportive of what I want."

"Give it time," I say. "He might come around and surprise you. But don't give up your dreams. Even if you have to take other classes, still keep practicing writing and doing what makes you happy. If writing is what you really want to do, you'll find a way to make it work. You're a smart girl. I'm confident about that."

"Thanks, Opal," she says. "Maybe you could talk to him." Her eyes light up with hope, but I shake my head.

"No, sweetie. This isn't something that I can get involved in. But feel free to contact me if you need some moral support."

"Thanks, Opal." She smiles, resigned.

"Now, if you'll excuse me, I have some more people to talk to. It was really good to see you, and thank you so much for coming today."

"Of course. Dad said it was important."

* * *

"MAN, I'm glad that we got the new location open today. But I'm happier to be here with you, Opal, on our way up to the mountain."

"Me too, sweetheart," I say, reaching over and putting my hand on his arm while he drives up King Mountain. We drive in comfortable silence. Usually, we talk the entire drive, but I know we're both talked out after the opening celebration today.

Ever since our first visit to King Mountain, we've been taking Waylon up on his offer to use one of the cabins for weekends. He said that unless it's the height of summer, there's always at least one available. We've come up for a weekend twice before, and we had such a good time that I convinced Champ that we needed to come up more often. It's wonderful to get away from everything and have it be just the two of us. The time we spend on the mountain has become so precious to me already. I still haven't met a lot of Waylon's guys who live on the mountain. But I know I will eventually.

"Here we are," Champ says, pulling into the driveway of one of the cabins.

There are lights already on in the windows. "Is somebody else here?" I ask, confused.

"No, it's just the two of us." Champ smiles, and I can see a twinkle in his eyes. "Let's get inside."

"What's going on?" I ask as I look around the cabin. My eyes widen with surprise. A fire crackles in the fireplace. An open bottle of wine sits on the table, along with a massive bouquet of flowers.

"I had Claudia help me with this," Champ admits, smiling at me.

"It's wonderful, Champ. Thank you." I move to Champ and he takes me in his arms, kissing me slow and deep.

The comfort and peace of being in his arms settle through me, and my desire flares to life as our kiss deepens. He slides his hands under my blouse and I arch my body into his.

"I've been wanting to touch you and be with you all day long, Opal," Champ says, his voice thick.

"I wanted the same thing," I say, reaching down and unzipping his jeans. "I guess you weren't kidding, were you?" I giggle when I discover how hard he is already.

"Babe, I'm always ready for you, and you know it." Champ grins at me, a wicked glint in his eye. "But first, let's sit on the couch and have a drink."

Champ leads me to the couch and I sip the glass of wine he gives me.

"Opal, you know I love you," Champ says, putting down his glass of wine and turning his body to me.

"I do." I smile. "I love you, too. Very much."

If you'd asked me at the beginning of summer if this is how I thought my life would be in autumn, I would have laughed. Yet the setup that Beth and Shelly put together worked, and now I'm happier than I ever imagined. Not a day that goes by when I don't silently thank them for helping Champ and me get together.

"Opal, since you entered my life, distracting me with your dresses in the gym, our relationship has redefined what I thought being in love would be. You constantly amaze me with your kindness and passion and your commitment to the community."

"Thank you, Champ. What is..."

"Please, let me finish," Champ says, putting his hand over mine. I nod, and he continues. "You make me happier than I thought I ever deserved. I owe you my life for not giving up on me, even when I tried to keep you at a distance. I never want to be apart from you ever again, Opal." Champ's voice wavers, and my heart pounds in my chest. "I know it's quick, but I don't need months or years to figure out how I feel."

"Oh, Champ," I whisper, understanding what he's saying.

Champ reaches into his pocket and pulls out a small, blue velvet box. He opens it, and a beautiful diamond ring twinkles in the light from the fireplace. "Will you do me the honor of being my wife?"

"Yes!" I say, not even hesitating for a moment.

I tremble with joy as he slides the ring on my finger. I pull him into a kiss and everything else in the world falls away as we fuse our promise to love each other for the rest of our lives.

* * *

THANK you so much for reading *Champion*!

If you enjoyed this book, please rate or review this book on Amazon, Goodreads, and Bookbub. Thank you!

This book is part of the Heartland Heroes series. This series is now complete! To catch up on the full series, please visit:

https://www.amazon.com/dp/B0BFRNY6CW

Do you want to read Roman's story? He's part of the crew at Rebel Autos, who will be featured in my next Heartland Heroes series. You can order Roman's book, **Dad Bod Rebel**, at:

https://www.amazon.com/dp/B0BT3FTQB2

Want to stay up to date on new releases, sales, and freebies! Join my newsletter!

http://eepurl.com/dh59Xr

For more Lana Love books, please visit:

https://www.amazon.com/Lana-Love/e/B078KKRB1T/

https://www.loveheartbooks.com